The Man from the Grave

Satanik Basu

Ukiyoto Publishing

DEDICATION

My love and attraction towards detective stories were from my childhood. As I am a Bengali language speaker, I started with "Feluda" a Bengali detective written by the great Satyajit Ray. As I grew up, slowly Sherlock Holmes, Hercule Poirot, Miss Marple, Byomkesh (another Bengali detective) and many more detective characters entered my life such as Jack Reacher. But the four detective characters that made impact in my life were Feluda, Sherlock Holmes, Hercule Poirot and Byomkesh. I never thought that I will write a book and create my own detective character. So, as I started writing, I kept in mind everything about my favourite detective writers and characters. The story is set in 1950's England. I'm strictly against the use of artificial intelligence in detective stories. So, this story doesn't have the use of any technology. This is the simple case of detection and deduction. In the words of the great "Hercule Poirot", using of the "little grey cells". I hope all the readers will love and enjoy this story. And in the end a huge thanks to Ukitiyo Publishing. I am so much grateful to them. Without their help this story would have never been published. Thanks Ukitiyo Publishing for this wonderful opportunity.
Satanik Basu

Contents

The Wood's chaos

England, London 1910. March 20:-

"Good afternoon Mr Woods" David Cunningham said. He was standing with a bouquet of flowers.

"Ah, David. Welcome son. Your friend is waiting for you at his room as usual. Well, he is wearing a special dress for today's occasion. At least that is what he told me. By the way nice flowers. I guess this is for Helen, right?" asked Brandon Woods.

"Yes Mr Woods. I brought these for Mrs Woods. Is she around?" asked David Cunningham.

"You may have to wait David. Because she is getting ready" Brandon Woods said.

"I will wait Sir. Oh, by the way sir, happy anniversary" David Cunningham greeted Brandon Woods with a nice smile on his face.

"Thank you very much David. Go. Enjoy the afternoon" Brandon Woods said went inside his room.

David Cunningham was waiting at the balcony for Helen Woods, wife of Brandon Woods. But he didn't have to wait longer. A few minutes later Helen Woods came out of her room and saw David Cunningham standing at the balcony with a beautiful bouquet of flowers.

"Happy anniversary Mrs Woods. I brought these for you" David Cunningham said and presented the bouquet of flowers to Helen Woods.

"Thank you my dear. Have you met Pete yet? He is wearing a special dress for us" Helen Woods said.

"Yes Mr Woods already told me that. I will meet him now. I was waiting for you. Have a wonderful party Mrs Woods. See you later" David Cunningham said and walked towards Peter Woods's room.

Peter Woods, the youngest son of Brandon and Helen Woods and perhaps the most polite person inside the entire Woods's family. He was getting ready in his room when the door was knocked.

"Who is it?" he asked.

"It is me Pete" David Cunningham said.

"Oh, come in my friend. I am almost done" Peter Woods said.

"Goodness gracious me. You look wonderful Pete. This dress is really gorgeous" David Cunningham said.

"I specially made it for mother's and father's anniversary" Peter Woods said.

"Hey, where is John, Mac and Rob? Are they ready for the party?" David Cunningham asked.

"Rob and Mac are ready and excited just like me. But John has no interest about this. I bet he won't even attain the party" Peter Woods said in a rather disappointed voice.

"What is wrong with John Pete?" David Cunningham asked.

"To be honest with you David, I have no idea what is going on with him. All I want him not to create any chaos today. Because there will be a lot of guests today from the different parts of the country. And some of them are very much respected in our society. It is all about the reputation and respect of my parents. I hope John won't create any chaos in front of all the guests" Peter Woods said.

"I hope that too my friend. Alright let's go to the party" David Cunningham said.

Peter Woods and David Cunningham both went downstairs to the party hall. Most of the guests were already arrived and started enjoying the party in their own ways. Rob and Mac Woods were standing at a corner of the hall with a glass of wine at each of their hands. Peter and David went towards them.

"Well John is nowhere to be seen as usual" Peter Woods said.

"He is in his room. I went to ask him to come. Just one afternoon. At least you can do this for our mother and father. But he denied as usual. He said he has no interest in this type of hypocrisy. Well, that's what a marriage anniversary party is all about according to him" Rob Woods said.

"May be he has a point" Mac Woods said.

"Oh please Mac. Don't take his side" Peter Woods said.

"I am taking his side? He is your favourite brother Pete. Not ours. You are the one who always cover his dirty works. I and Rob don't. We never take his side" Mac Woods said in a cringe voice.

"Alright now don't argue over these things. Let's enjoy the party" David Cunningham said.

Slowly the party hall began to fill with different voices and cents of perfumes as more guests arrived at the venue. A group of musicians were playing a wonderful tune to make the party more lively and beautiful. But to be honest no body was listening to them. Because everybody was busy in whether drinking or eating and gossiping about each other's lives. Unlike a concert musicians don't get value in these type of parties.

Peter Woods was about to say something when he spotted John Woods, his elder brother came downstairs and went inside the kitchen. Peter was a little surprised.

"What?" Rob Woods asked.

"John came down and went inside the kitchen. He looked in a bit hurry" Peter Woods said.

"What does he has to do in kitchen?" asked Mac Woods.

"I don't know. Let's go and take a look" Peter Woods said.

And as all four of them were about to go, a very loud scream came from the kitchen. Everybody heard it. Some of the guests got startled. Even the musicians stopped playing their instruments. Before even realising what happened, John Woods came out of the kitchen, looked at the guests for a moment and then ran upstairs. Brandon Woods, his wife, his three sons and David Cunningham went inside the kitchen. A woman name Kathrine was wiping on the shoulder of another kitchen maid. She was the one who screamed and the other woman, Rebeca was trying to console her.

"What happened Rebeca" asked Brandon Woods.

Nobody said a word.

"Tell me what happened" Brandon Woods asked again.

"It is your Son Sir. John. He was forcing Kathrine to do.., you know what I mean Sir" said Rebeca.

In a certain moment Brandon Woods's face turned into something else.

"Goodness gracious me. This boy never gives me a day to breath properly. I can't allow this" Brandon Woods said in peevish voice.

Perhaps Peter realised what was about to happen. So he quickly moved towards his father and said—

"Look father. It may not be exactly what it looks"

"Really Pete? Do you think these two women are lying? Look at Kathrine's face. What do you see? Lie or fear?

Stop covering and protecting your brother" Brandon Woods almost shouted out loud.

"Let me talk to him father. I can make him realise" Peter Woods said in a requesting voice.

"Enough talking Pete. I have tolerated a lot. It ends today. This won't go unpunished" Brandon Woods said went towards the stairs and shouted—

"John. Get down here now. I won't ask a second time."

John Woods came down in a pin drop silence. Brandon Woods told Rebeca to bring Kathrine to him.

"Did you force her to fulfil your.., goodness me. I can't even pronounce those words. Did you force her or did you not? Answer me" Brandon Woods was boiling in anger.

"Yes father. I did" John Woods replied in a low voice.

"You bloody brute of a man. You forced an innocent girl to do your dirty work? Is this what I taught you John? Look what you have done. You insulted me, your mother, and your brothers in front of all these people. Everything I built in all these years, the legacy, reputation and pride all are destroyed now because of you. I have tolerated you enough John. But not anymore. Take your belongings and leave this house forever and never to come back" Brandon Woods said.

"Father, please don't do this. I will talk to him. Please father" Peter Woods begged.

"Please Brandon. Listen to your son. I know John made a mistake. But don't kick him out. He is our son.

Where will he go?" Helen Woods couldn't hold back her tears.

"No Helen. I made up my decision. He has to leave" Brandon Woods said.

John Woods looked at his father's face and ran upstairs. Peter Woods followed him

"Listen John. Father got angry. That's why he said it. He never meant it. He loves you. You know that right?" Peter Woods asked.

"He doesn't love me little brother. He never loved me. Because of you I lasted this long in this house. But I don't want to be a burden on your shoulder anymore. So I will go. But I won't forget this. My time will come and I will get what is right fully mine" John Woods said and went down stairs.

"I Will never this forget this father. I will rise one day. I will have my revenge" John Woods said and walked out of the house in anguish.

The day which was supposed to be a very much colourful day because of the ceremony, turned into a very much negative and perhaps the worst day in the history of Woods's family. A few friends of Brandon Woods's tried to sooth him and Mrs Woods. But that didn't work out properly. Peter Woods was still looking at the doorway.

"Staring at the doorway won't bring him back Pete. He got what he deserved" Brandon Woods said.

"No father. He didn't deserved this. You never liked him because he didn't follow your path like all of us did. You always wanted him to look after your business. But he had other ambitions and there is nothing wrong in it. I kept my mouth shut for a long time. You have to listen to me now father. You made loads of mistakes. If you don't believe me, then ask mother. And one of those mistakes was not to love and support John what he needed all the time. I always respected his life choices. Because among all the brothers, he was the only one who has the courage and guts of living his life in his own terms.

I know what he had done can't go unpunished. But this was not the punishment he deserved. You will regret this one day father. Did you ever think about us? Mother? Did you ever think about what we want? No. You didn't. It is all about you isn't it father? He is your son. May be you forgot that" Peter Woods said and went out of the house.

David Cunningham went out with Peter Woods.

England, London 1910. March 27:-

The entire Woods's family was sitting on the bedroom of Helen Woods. Helen Woods was lying on the bed and Brandon Woods was sitting beside her holding her right hand.

"I shouldn't have let him go" Brandon Woods said in a sobbing voice.

"I should have listened to you and your mother Pete. I shouldn't have let him go. Otherwise this would have never happened" Brandon Woods said.

"Mother loved John more than any one of us. She was suffering father. She couldn't live like this. It is not your fault" Peter Woods said.

Brandon Woods broke down into tears. The lifeless body of Helen Woods was enlightening upon all the mistakes. The departure of her most beloved son was a fatal blow to her. A blow she couldn't tolerate any more. The helplessness of not having her son to herself slowly took away the last hope from her life. And finally after seven days of endless mental suffering, she took her last breath and left a huge obligation upon the entire family of reuniting the brotherhood again. Half of the London was present at her funeral.

"You were looking for me father?" Peter Woods asked.

Brandon Woods was sitting on his favourite couch in his bedroom with a glass of scotch in his hand. He replied—

"Yes my son. Seat here. I have something important to discuss with you."

"Why don't you leave this habit of drinking father? Slowly it will become an addiction you know that right?" Peter Woods said in a worrying voice.

"Don't worry about me Pete. Now listen to me very carefully. There is something I never told you about our family. Only I and Helen knew and somehow John got to know about this. I will tell you what it is but you have to promise me that you won't tell anyone. Not even your brothers. It important that it stays as a secret. Can you do that for me?" Brandon Woods asked.

"Of course I can. Now tell me what it is" Peter Woods said.

Brandon Woods explained everything to his son. As much as he was listening to his father, he was getting astounded.

"Goodness gracious me. But how did John get to know about this?" Peter Woods asked.

"I think he must have heard when I and your mother were discussing about this. Listen Pete. I had done things about which I am proud of. But I had also done things about which I am really ashamed of. I can't stay here Pete" Brandon Woods said.

"What? What do you mean you can't stay here? You just can't abandon us" Peter Woods said.

"No my son. I am the reason for all this chaos. Because of my one wrong decision you lost your brother and mother. I am leaving London. I will go as far as possible. Away from all of you" Brandon Woods said.

"But what will we do? I, Rob and Mac? We went motherless a few days ago and now we are about to be fatherless? Please father. Don't leave us" Peter Woods pleaded.

"It is too late my son. I have to go" Brandon Woods said.

"Then at least tell me where you are going" Peter Woods said.

"I don't know yet. But I will let you know once I get there. I will write letter to you my son and I will take that thing with me. It is not safe here. Because if John is right about his words, he will come back for this. That's why it is not safe here" Brandon Woods said.

"How will I suppose to explain this to Rob and Mac?" Peter Woods asked.

"You will find a way my son. You always do. I will leave tomorrow morning. You can go now. I need to sleep. I have a long journey tomorrow. A journey to the unknown. Good night Pete" Brandon Woods said and closed his eyes.

Peter Woods stood there for a minute or so before shutting the door on his way out of the room.

The Dark Spirit

ngland, London, 1950:-

Peter Woods was standing on his balcony with a glass of Brandy in his hand. It was half past twelve in the night. His servant Luke already went back home. He lives near Peter Woods's house. Peter Woods, the youngest and the last decadent of the royal Woods's family. He was the youngest of the four brothers. In the last two years rest of his three brothers died mysteriously. He was thinking about his three dead brothers. How brutal their deaths were. All of them were murdered by somebody but in different locations. The police did investigate all of the three murders but they never found the person who did these massacre. Peter Woods was thinking about Rob, the eldest one. He was close to Rob. Rob was the only bother among four of them who understood Peter more than anyone in the family. Peter loved him a lot. His death was an unbearable pain to Peter. All those wonderful moments he spent with his brother had slowly began to occupy his mind and very soon his vision became blurred.

It was the pain of losing Rob, his most beloved brother was coming in the form of tears. Peter Woods couldn't control himself. Or maybe he didn't want to.

"Oh dear Rob. My brother. My poor brother. You are the only one I had left. Yet God took you away from me."

His entire body was shaking. He couldn't stand any more. So he went down on one knee. Peter Woods was breathing heavily. He was there for quite a few minutes. Then finally he calmed himself down and stood up. As he was about to go inside suddenly something grabbed his attention. Someone was walking near the wall of the garden. But that is impossible. Because the entire compound is surrounded by high walls. So it is impossible to jump over and come inside. Peter Woods kept on looking. Yes, someone is walking by the wall. A man. Tall and wearing a hat and an overcoat. But the behaviour of that man seemed familiar to Peter Woods. He is very much familiar with the nature of walking of that man. So he looked carefully to see that man and the moment he saw him, his face became pale and his hands started shaking. He started to breath heavily again. Even in this cold weather he was sweating. He knows this man. This is his brother John Woods who was found dead a year ago.

But how is this possible? Peter Woods buried his brother himself. Now his entire body started shaking. Peter Woods doesn't believe in supernatural power or paranormal activity but whatever was happening, was happening in front of his eyes. Yes. Indeed that man was John Woods. It seems like he is back from the grave. That man came towards the balcony where Peter Woods was standing and stared directly towards him.

For a second his vision became blurred and immediately he fell on the ground and became unconscious. Around five in the morning Peter Woods regained his consciousness. He had no idea for how long he was unconscious. But as he stood up, everything that happened last night came back to his mind again. Somehow he controlled himself, went to his bedroom and drank an entire bottle of Brandy.

Around eight in the morning his servant Luke came. Peter Woods was still lying on his bed, eyes closed with a hand on his forehead. This looked a little unusual to Luke. Because Peter Woods is an early riser. He normally wakes up around 5 in the morning and goes to morning walk around six every day. He always knocks Luke's door like an alarm clock on his way back to the house. This routine never changes. But for some reason Peter Woods didn't knock Luke's door today morning. And that's why he woke up late. So he went inside the bedroom when he didn't see his master at the drawing room.

"My God. Are you alright Sir?" Luke asked. He was a bit worried.

"Who is that?" Peter Woods almost sat up in a hurry.

"Oh Luke. My dear God. I thought" Peter Woods stopped for moment to breath.

"You thought who Sir?" Luke asked.

"What happened? Is everything alright? You didn't go to morning walk today? Please tell me Sir what's going on" Luke pleaded.

"I will Luke. But give a glass of water" Peter Woods said.

Luke gave him a glass of water. Peter Woods drank two more glasses of water after the first and then began to say whatever he saw last night—

"Something unthinkable happened last night Luke. I was standing in the balcony with a glass of brandy and was thinking about my brother Rob. I got a bit emotional but eventually calmed myself down and as I was about to go inside I saw a man who was coming towards the balcony. Now you know Luke that is impossible. Because no one can get inside because of the high walls. Yet that man somehow came inside. It was too dark. So I couldn't see his face until he came closer to the balcony. Once he came, I recognised him. It was, It was" Peter Woods couldn't speak any more.

"It was who Sir?" Luke asked.

"It was John Woods. My dead brother" Peter Woods said and closed his eyes in horror.

"What? John Woods? What are you saying Sir?" Luke was looking at his master with a lot of disbelief.

"I am telling the truth Luke. It was John" Peter Woods almost screamed.

"Please calm down Sir and think in cold head. How is this possible? We both went to his funeral. You buried him himself in front of everybody. How in the earth is he still be alive?" Luke asked.

"So you are saying it wasn't him" Peter Woods asked angrily.

"All I am saying that there was a man but certainly not him. Sir you were drunk and emotional at the same time. It is quite easy to overthink and hallucinate. Because this is not possible. You certainly don't believe in ghost do you? Because I don't. And if I agree with you of whatever you have seen last night, ghost is the only explanation. Please Sir. Think about it" Luke said.

"So if I agree with your words, then you may say that there wasn't anybody at all. Because I was hallucinating right? Are you even listening to your words Luke? I would never have said this rubbish if it wasn't for real. It was him. Trust me. Now I don't know whether it was some kind of supernatural incident or not but I saw him by my own eyes. It was real" Peter Woods said.

Luke looked at his master for a second and then said—

"Alright Sir. I believe you. But you know Sir indeed it is very hard to believe that John Woods came back from the grave. Anyway, what are you going to do about it?"

"I want to you stay tonight with me. He came last night. He will come tonight too. Will you stay with me Luke?" Peter Woods asked.

"Yes Sir I will. I want to see everything" Luke said.

Luke stayed throughout the day with Peter Woods. He constantly kept an eye on his master. Peter Woods looked a bit unstable throughout the day and as it was getting dark, he started to panic a bit. There was a few times when he really wanted to breakdown in tears but somehow managed himself. Despite of everything it was still an incident not to believe. Slowly night fell and it started to get dark. It was just a normal night like every other night but perhaps because of what Peter Woods told to Luke, he felt a bit uneasy. Both of them spent the entire evening sitting on the couch in the drawing room. They hardly spoke with each other. As the clock ticked to eleven, Peter Woods said—

"Let's get ready."

Half an hour later Peter Woods and Luke came out of the house. They looked around to assess the situation and then went towards a tree and hide themselves behind it. Twelve o'clock in the night. Peter Woods and Luke were still hiding behind a tree in the garden. After a few minutes Luke became a little restless.

"Nobody is coming, Sir. Please believe me. It was a hallucination. He died. We both saw know this. You buried him yourself. I was there at his funeral. It is impossible Sir. Please listen to me. Let's go back inside. It's too cold to be out here in the middle of the night" Luke said.

"Just a few minutes Luke. He will come. I don't care whether he comes as a spirit or in flesh, but he will come. So please wait" Peter Woods said.

Luke was about to say something but right then Peter Woods tapped Luke's back and said—

"Look right there Luke. You believe me now?"

Peter Woods was pointing his finger towards the balcony. Luke tried to see in the dark. A man was standing there. But not looking at the house. He was looking towards that tree where Peter and Luke were hiding. It was like the man already knew that they are hiding somewhere there. Luke never saw John in flesh. All he remembered is the face of John Woods from a photo. Slowly that man was coming towards them. Now Luke saw the face of that man and he couldn't believe his eyes. Indeed it was John Woods.

"Dear God. It is him" Luke said. His voice was crumbling. We will be dead if we stay here. Run Sir. Get inside the house" Luke whispered.

Both of Peter Woods and Luke stood up and ran towards the house in fear. As they were entering the house they heard the guffaw of John Woods. It sounded like a roar of a tiger.

"Do you believe me now?" asked Peter Woods.

"My God. It was him. But how is this possible? He was dead" Luke said.

"I don't know Luke. I can't think of anything. See Luke, two things are possible. Whether it is the spirit of my brother or he is not dead" Peter Woods said.

"Not dead? Do you have any idea what you have just said? If it wasn't him then whose dead body have you buried?" Luke asked.

"I guess we both have to find that out. Something is happening. I need to find out what is going on." Peter Woods said.

"But how?" Luke asked.

"I will find a way out. I need to talk to David. He might be able to help me" Peter Woods said.

They spent rest of the night locked themselves in Peter Woods's bedroom. Though a few times Luke sneaked through the window to see whether the spirit of John Woods is still there or not. They couldn't sleep throughout the night. Every single time they closed their eyes John Woods came to haunt them.

In the next morning Peter Woods called his oldest friend David Cunningham. Cunningham came around ten in the morning. Peter Woods was seating on his drawing room.

"Is everything alright Pete? You sounded a bit tensed over the phone" Cunningham said.

"Take a seat David" Peter Woods said.

His eyes were red and face was pale due to that terrible incident happened last night. David Cunningham realised that something is wrong.

"What is going on Pete? Tell me. You are looking horrible. Didn't you sleep last night?" Cunningham asked.

Peter Woods called Luke and asked him to stay there and then said—

"I will tell you everything and you have to believe me David. Because I won't be lying."

Peter Woods explained everything to his friend. Luke verified it and said at first he also didn't believe his master but after seeing everything last night now he does believe that whether it is the spirit of John woods or he is in flesh himself.

David Cunningham was speechless after hearing what Peter Woods had to say. It was hard for him to fathom. He said—

"I don't' know what to say Pete. How can I explain this to anybody? See Pete, you know that I don't believe in supernatural power or paranormal incidents. Because things like these doesn't exists. So if it wasn't John then whose body we buried?"

"I don't know David. All I know that something is wrong. Something is not adding up. Anyway have you heard the name Wilfred Dankworth?" Peter Woods asked.

"Of course I heard. That famous detective who solved the double murder case of Harold Carter and Julia Wilson. The entire England have heard his name. Why?" David Cunningham asked.

"Listen David. I don't think I will stay alive for long. John will kill me. And if this happens, you will go to Mr Dankworth. He can help you" Peter Woods said.

"Stop talking nonsense Pete. Nothing will happen to you. And even if there is a chance of your death, why don't we try to stop it. Why don't we go to him now?" David Cunningham asked.

"I need to talk to him" Peter Woods said.

"Talk to whom?" David Cunningham asked.

"Talk to John" Peter Woods said.

"Are you out of your mind? You just said that he might kill you and you want to talk to him?" Cunningham asked.

"I need to confront him David. There is no other way. I need to know why has he came back. And if he is still alive, then whose body we buried? I need all these answers and I can't have them sitting here. I have to confront him" Peter Woods said.

"But how will you find him?" asked David Cunningham.

"He will find me. I believe he kept an eye on me. He follows everywhere I go. Sooner or later he will give me a hint. Look David. There was only two men inside the house last night. He could have easily come inside and killed both me and Luke. But he didn't. He had that chance the day before yesterday too. I went unconscious watching his face. Yet he didn't kill me. I believe all he wanted is to scare me. I need to know why" Peter Woods said.

"Alright. Then in that case I am going with you. Because this is suicide Pete. I can't let you go alone. But one thing I don't understand. What will he get by scaring you or killing you? That incident happened a long time ago Pete. Your father told him to leave the house. You had nothing to do with it. In fact you were the only one who actually tried to convince your father to not to let him go. So he should be angry on your father, not on you" David Cunningham said.

"Then why did he come back David? Why? He came back for a reason. I need to find it. And the only way to find it is to meet him. I know it is risky. But I don't have any other choice" Peter Woods said.

"But where will you meet him?" David Cunningham asked.

"Somewhere quiet I guess. Because he choose to visit the house in the middle of the night. So if I go somewhere quiet in the middle of the night, he will follow me there. He won't let that chance go away. I think Regents Park will be the best place for that meeting" Peter Woods said.

"Alright Pete I will follow you from behind. Just let me know when you will leave" David Cunningham said.

"I will David. But please remember, if anything happens to me, go straight to Wilfred Danlworth" Peter Woods said.

"I will Pete. Don't worry" David Cunningham said and walked out of the door.

Peter Woods was sitting in front of the fireplace on his favourite couch. It was twelve o'clock in the night. His servant Luke just brought a cup of hot coffee for his master.

"Are you really going to go, Sir?" Luke asked.

"Yes Luke. I have to" said Peter Woods.

"But you didn't inform Mr Cunningham. If you are going alone, then who will watch over you?" Luke said.

"If John sees that I am not alone he will never come. See Luke I said earlier, he is watching our house day and night. He definitely has seen David coming into my house. So if David comes with me tonight he will never show up. I have to go alone" Peter Woods said.

"But it is too risky Sir. Then take me with you. He doesn't know me" Luke said.

"He didn't previously. But he knows you now. Because he saw you last night. It will be alright Luke. Nothing will happen to me. And it is between the two brothers. I don't want to drag you into this matter. That's why I can't take you with me. It has to be me Luke. It has to be me." Peter Woods said.

"Why is it so important for you to go to Regent's park in the middle of the night? You don't even know whether it is a spirit or a man in flesh. He is haunting you wherever you go, even inside the house. Why are you risking your life?" Luke asked.

"It is important Luke. You won't understand. Anyway I have to go. You don't need to wait around. Go to your bed. And don't worry. I will be alright" Peter Woods said and walked out through the main door of his house.

Luke waited until Peter Woods completely went out of his sight and then slowly he closed the door.

Peter Woods was dressed in black. He was walking to the Regent's park. The distance between his house and Regent's park is one kilometre. He was walking slowly. It took around 15-20 minutes for him to reach the Regent's park. All the gates were closed. So he had to jump over a wall to get inside. Though he was fourty years old, jumping over a wall wasn't that hard for him. Once he got inside the Regent's park, he waited for a few minutes. It was twelve past thirty on the clock. Though it was the middle of the night, yet the entire park was quite visible due to bright moonlight. So Peter Woods didn't turn on the torch. He took a good look around the place and then started walking towards his left. After walking for five minutes he finally sat on a bench. He again checked the watch. It was twelve forty five on the clock. Peter Woods started to get restless. He sat there for ten more minutes and then decided to leave the place. As he was about to stand up and leave, a heavy voice came from behind.

"Leaving too soon?"

Peter Woods couldn't turn around. He started to sweat. That unknown voice was heard again—

"I asked you a question and I expect an answer. Please turn around Pete."

Peter Woods slowly turned around and took two steps backward in horror. He couldn't believe his own eyes.

He was breathing heavily. His eyes were almost popping out.

"Did you see a ghost Pete?" A man came out from the dark. He was wearing black overcoat and a black hat. He had a knife in his right hand.

"How is this possible? You were dead. I buried you myself" Peter Woods said in a horrifying voice. His entire body was shivering in fear.

"Yet you see I am still alive" said John Woods.

"Alright John. Why have you come back? And what do you want from me? You didn't bring me out here alone in the middle of the night for a family gossip I guess?" asked Peter Woods.

"Your sense of humour haven't dried up yet brother. Even in this age, Impressive" said John Woods.

"Did you kill Rob and Mac? They were your brothers too John. So am I. You are going to kill me just like them? Aren't you brother after getting what you want? Answer the damn question" Peter Woods screamed in agony.

"May be I will spare your life if you give me what I want" said that John Woods.

"I know what you want John. But you will never get it. Doesn't matter how much you try. It is not here in the, aahhh", Peter Woods couldn't end his words. A sharp knife entered inside his stomach. He fell on the ground. He was still alive and barely breathing. John Woods sat down beside his brother on one knee and asked—

"Were you saying something little brother? Oh I am so sorry, I forgot that I just pierced a knife into your stomach. Listen Pete, I don't need you to tell me where it is. I will find it myself. All I needed to know that whether it exists or not. And you just confirmed that it does exists. I wasn't blessed like you Pete. You were a good boy throughout your life. You had all the love from mother and father. And all I got is hatred. It ends here today. So you see I don't need you alive anymore. Any last word brother?" asked John Woods.

Even in this intolerable pain there was a smile on Peter Woods's face.

"Why the hell are you smiling? You are about to die" said John Woods.

"After you left us, a few days later mother died. Our father couldn't take it. So he left London and went somewhere else. There he married again. They had a child. You see, big brother I am not the only one remaining. There is one more. You are not going to get what you want. Because that child has the right to claim the same and I won't tell you where our father went and the name of that child" Peter Woods said and then slowly fell in the lap of death.

"Pete, Pete" John Woods screamed. But it was too late. Peter Woods was already dead.

"I will find that child at any cost and I will have what is rightfully mine" John Woods said walked out of the Regent's park leaving Peter Woods's dead body under the shining moonlight.

Grief and Guilt

It was twenty past twelve in the night. David Cunningham was sitting on his favourite couch with a glass of brandy. He couldn't sleep. He was constantly thinking about his friend and Wood's family. From his childhood he was very much close to that family. Though he was a bit less in terms of wealth and reputation but the Wood's family never let those differences come between their relationships. Throughout all these years he had some wonderful memories with them. He was thinking about all of that. How beautiful those days were. He was closest to Peter Woods. But sometimes Rob and Mack would join them in catching squirrel in their backyard. David Cunningham's vision got blurred. A drop of tear fell into his glass of brandy. Because all those elegant memories flew in front of his eyes in a flash.

"No. I can't let Pete go alone" he said to himself. He knew that his friend won't listen to him. So he will convince Luke, Pete's servant to let him know when Pete leaves the house. He would wait there hidden and will see the entire thing through. He decided to go to Peter Wood's house next day early morning to check on him and visit Luke's house on his way back to home. It was ten past one on the clock. David Cunningham finished the remaining brandy and went to sleep.

It was six thirty on the clock next morning. David Cunningham was getting ready. As he was about to come out of his house, somebody knocked his front door and screamed his name.

"Mr Cunningham. Mr Cunningham".

He recognised that voices. It was Luke's. It was loud and full of grief. David Cunningham's right hand shivered a little for a moment. He took a step back. Luke was continuously knocking the door and screaming his name. Finally David Cunningham gathered courage and opened the door. Luke rushed inside and broke into tears. David Cunningham couldn't look at him. By then he realised exactly what happened.

"He killed him. He killed him Sir" Luke said and fell unconscious on the floor. David Cunningham ran towards him but he couldn't hold him. Because he himself was unstable. Somehow he carried Luke to his bed and tried to bring him back. Luke woke up a few minutes later and was looking at David Cunningham with an unanswerable face.

"How" David Cunningham asked.

"He was stabbed brutally Sir" Luke was stammering.

"Who told you" David Cunningham asked.

"A constable came to the house this morning. The park cleaner saw his dead body first and called the police. I told him not to go alone Sir. But he didn't listen. I pleaded him to inform you but he denied. I even begged him to take me with him. But he was so stubborn Sir, he didn't listen a single word I said. All he said that if he doesn't go alone John will never show up. I knew something would go wrong. Oh God. What will we do now?" Luke's last few words got covered with his sobbing voice.

David Cunningham put his hand on Luke's head. Luke slowly looked towards him.

"I lost the last person who cared for me Luke and so do you. I don't know how we will cope up with this but at this point we have to stay strong. I see this through Luke. I won't stop until I find that bloody haggard. This time he isn't getting away. But right now we have to go to the police station and see what they have found" David Cunningham said.

"And what about that detective he told you?" Luke asked.

"Wilfred Dankworth. I will go to him too. But first we have to go to the police station" David Cunningham said.

David Cunningham and Luke were sitting in Raymond Wright's office. Raymond Wright, the chief detective of Scotland Yard was the investigation officer of this case. David Cunningham explained everything to Raymond Wright and Luke verified it.

"Well, this is unreal. I know you are telling what you have seen and heard but both of you can realise that it is very hard to believe. I mean a spirit? Come on Mr Cunningham. Do you even believe in this nonsense?

Look all I can understand after hearing all of this that was Peter Wood's brother John Woods. May be he didn't die. Because none of you saw his body. You, he and Peter Woods went to his funeral but he was already inside the casket by then. How definitely can you confirm that it was him? It looks like John Woods killed someone else and showed the entire World that he died. Well as far as I can understand he needed to be dead in order to return to London and kill your friend. But the question is why and for what? His brother didn't throw him out of the house. His father did. Then why did he take revenge on his brother. I think there is something else. Something so important that he came back and killed your friend. Do you know anything important about that family Mr Cunningham?" Raymond Wright asked.

"No Sir. Though I was close to that family but these are internal family matter. Why would they discuss these thing in front of me or with me" David Cunningham said.

"Well Mr Cunningham, we will try to do the best from our side. But in the meantime I would advise to you consult this with a dear friend of mine. Mr Wilfred Dankworth. I hope you heard his name. He single handedly solved the murder of Harold Carter and Julia Wilson a few months ago" Raymond Wright said.

"Of course I heard his name. In fact Pete told me to go to him if anything happens" David Cunningham said.

"Go to him. He has an ability to deduct matters like nothing. He can help you more than anyone" Raymond Wright said.

The police released Peter Wood's body on that evening. His funeral was on the next day. Almost half of London attended Peter wood's funeral.

"England has lost another great man today. He was a man of honour and a man with a golden heart. We all know what he did for this city after his father departed London. He continued the charity for the poor and helpless people. He was a wonderful man and a better friend. I was no way near to his fame and wealth. Yet he never let me felt that for one moment. May god rest his soul" David Cunningham said.

A Brutal Murder

"**G**ood morning Mr Bennett."

"Ah, Willie. Good morning. You don't forget a day do you?" I asked. Willie Brooke is my good neighbour. A young chap with a very good sense of humour.

"No Mr Bennett. I don't" Willie said.

I was sitting on a chair in my garden with a cup coffee and the newspaper. This is how I spend my morning. And just like every other day Willie joined me.

"How is your detective friend?" Willie asked.

"He is alright" I said.

"You know Mr Bennett, I have been living here for the last one and a half years. But not for a second in my life I understood that Mr Wilfred Dankworth is a detective. In fact the entire Wiveliscombe had no idea about it. All we knew is that he is a musician" Willie said.

I smiled at him and was about to say something, right then Willie said—

"There she comes."

"Who?" I asked.

"Evelyn Mr Bennett. Who else? The most beautiful lady in the world. Isn't she the reason why you choose to stay in the garden at this exact time?" Willie asked.

Even though Willie was right, yet I felt a little embarrassed by his words. Because Evelyn would be at my daughter's age if I would have ever married. That is why I was embarrassed. But that doesn't take away the truth. Indeed Evelyn Foster is one of the most beautiful girl I have ever seen in my life.

"Good morning Willie. Good morning Mr Bennett." I was thinking all those words until I heard Evelyn's beautiful voice.

"Good morning Evelyn" both I and Willie said at the same time and then we looked at each other.

Evelyn smiled and said—

"How is Mr Dankworth Mr Bennett? Is he not around?"

"No Evelyn. He went to the river side. You know his habit of morning walk. He will come back exactly at 8.30 A.M." I said.

"You look beautiful as usual" Willie said.

Evelyn smiled and left for the church. As soon as she left I said—

"What was that Willie?"

"What?" Willie asked.

"You just said that she is looking so beautiful" I said.

"Isn't she? I think she is. And that was a complement" Willie said.

"I know Willie. But please remember she is about to be married to another man" I said.

"I know that Mr Bennett. Anyway, have a good day" Willie said and left in anguish. I came inside my room. Wilfred was not home yet. So I decided to take a nap. It was a Sunday morning.

I went to Wilfred's house in the evening. We both were sitting in Wilfred's drawing room. As usual Wilfred was playing his evergreen blues music on his guitar and I was reading a book while enjoying the sounds of strings. The case of Harold Carter and Julia Wilson is still fresh news in every newspaper of England. This case made a huge impact on the people of this country. The aftermath of the Second World War was just passing by and on top of that, the brutal murder of Harold Carter and Julia Wilson shook the entire nation. People started doubting the person living next door. But on the positive side of it, my dear friend Mr Wilfred Dankworth, a musician and a private detective, grabbed the attention of the entire country towards him including the British government. Wilfred's detection and deduction process were much appreciated and very soon he started working with the British government unofficially.

"You are still thinking about her aren't you Richard?" Wilfred asked.

He was playing his guitar nonstop for the last five minutes. I looked at him. Though I was taken by surprise by his question but didn't show any of it on my face.

"Still thinking about her means? Who are you talking about? I didn't understand" I said with a solemn face as much as possible.

"You didn't understand or didn't try to understand?" Wilfred asked in his usual mockery voice.

"No I didn't understand" I said.

"You were thinking about Evelyn. I told you Richard, she is much younger than you and very happy with her future husband" Wilfred said.

"Who told you I was thinking about Evelyn? In fact I wasn't. I was thinking about the tragic death of Harold Carter and Julia Wilson" I said.

"Really? You were thinking about their tragic death while reading a romantic book? Well, I thought that is impossible" Wilfred said.

Only then I realized that indeed I am reading a romantic book which is rather unusual for me because I rarely show interest in reading romantic books and Wilfred knows this.

I looked at him with a smile and asked—

"How did you know it was Evelyn?"

"Very simple. Ever since we came back from London you started talking to her again. Every morning you come out of your house and wait in your garden just to talk to her. You know at what time she goes to the church don't you? So you wait in your garden until she comes back. I have seen your face Richard. You become extremely happy whenever you see her. Please don't write any romantic poem for her this time Richard" Wilfred said.

I smiled at Wilfred because that is the only thing I could have done. Well, to be honest, Wilfred was right. Evelyn Foster was slowly taking possession of my heart again. I said—

"But Wilfred, you know that I stopped thinking about her."

"Of course you did my dear Watson but that was a different time. Then, your grey matter was busy in thinking about the case of Harold Carter and Julia Wilson. So you didn't have the time to think about her. But now, when you have nothing serious to think about, she came back into your heart. Again" Wilfred said.

"Yes she did. So what? I like to" I stopped.

"You like to what? Imagining that she is yours?" Wilfred laughed in his loudest voice.

"Can we talk about something else please?" I asked.

"Of course we can. But to do that, you need to stop thinking about her" Wilfred said and laughed again.

"You know Wilfred you will never understand this. Anyway, I am leaving. I have some work to do" I said and stood up from the couch.

"Don't dream about her at night" Wilfred said.

I threw the book towards him and left the room.

The next morning I stood in my garden as usual to talk to Evelyn. I can understand Wilfred's concern about my possessiveness about Evelyn but I like it this way. I tried to explain this to Wilfred so many times but he never understood. I spent the rest of the day like every other day. It was four o'clock in the afternoon when Wilfred shouted my name from his window.

"Richard. Richard" he shouted.

It was so loud that I had to answer immediately. I ran out of my house and came to the garden.

"What? Why are you shouting like this mate? What's the matter?" I asked.

"Come to my home. I have to tell you something. Something very important. Come right now" Wilfred said.

So I went to his home in a hurry. I ran up the stairs instead of walking and went straight to his drawing room and asked—

"What's going on? Is everything alright?"

"Everything is perfect my dear Watson. What happened is that we have a visitor. A client. I thought you should know" Wilfred said very politely.

"Good afternoon Mr Cunningham. This is Richard. My friend and assistant. Just like Watson" Wilfred said and laughed at his own humour.

"I already know about both of you. In fact the entire country knows about both of your heroic work. The way you solved Harold Carter and Julia Wilson's murder is unbelievable Mr Dankworth" Mr Cunningham said.

"Thank you Mr Cunningham. Alright now tell me the reason of your visit" Wilfred said.

"Did you read this news?" Mr Cunningham handed Wilfred the newspaper and pointed towards a particular place.

I and Wilfred both took a look at the news.

"Brutal murder at the Regent's park. Peter Woods, the youngest and the last descendant of the Royal Woods family was found dead in the middle of the Regent's park. He was brutally murdered. According to Scotland Yard the incident happened around midnight."

"Of course Mr Cunningham. We both read it" Wilfred said.

"Peter was my closest friend Mr Danlworth. There is a big background to this matter. Actually I know who killed him. But what I am about you may seem unreal but that is exactly what happened. I want you to investigate Peter's murder. Scotland Yard is taking over the case. Before coming here I went to Scotland Yard. Chief detective Raymond Wright is in charge and just like Pete, he also told me to consult you about this matter. Actually Pete knew that there is chance that he may die and if that happens, he wanted me to come to you" Mr Cunningham said.

"What? He knew he will die. Then why didn't he tried to stop it?" Wilfred asked.

"Well, that is what I am about to tell you" Mr Cunningham started to say—

"My name is David Cunningham. I knew the Woods's family from my childhood. Despite being one of the oldest and royal families of England, they never divided people by their caste. At least they didn't do it with me. Peter was the youngest of four brothers. The eldest was Rob. Then John and Mac. Their father was one of the most respected person in the entire London, Mr Brandon Woods. His mother, Helen Woods was also a very kind hearted woman. All of the brothers were polite and kind hearted except John. John wasn't like that at all. He was rough, rude and brutal in nature. There was an incident. It happened when I was 15 years old. So almost 40 years ago. It was Peter's birthday. His father arranged a house party that afternoon. All the distinguished people from different part of England and their families were invited.

Everything was going perfectly alright until John created a chaotic situation in front of all the guests. He was misbehaving with one of the waitresses of the house. He got very drunk and couldn't control himself. He was forcing the waitress to do something unacceptable. John was heavily punished for that. Mr

Brandon Woods kicked him out the house. But he took that punishment very seriously. He John left the house and never came back. His mother Helen Woods couldn't tolerate this. So a few days after John's departure she died of a heart attack. That period of time was very much tough for the Woods's family. Brandon Woods slowly became addicted and one day he also left the house. Only Peter knew where he had gone. No one else."

David Cunningham stopped for a minute. He was breathing heavily. I gave him a cup of coffee. He took one sip and then started again—

"Around a year ago I left London and went to Lancashire. A few days after I went there, I received a letter from Peter. The letter contained the demise of Rob Woods. He was murdered just like Peter. But not in London. Rob left England soon after his father left the house. He was living in Australia. Peter couldn't bring back his dead body. So he was buried there. Then five months later two more deaths occurred. John and Mac both were murdered in similar fashion."

"Where were they murdered?" Wilfred asked?

"Here in England" Mr Cunningham said.

"John too? Did he come back to London?" I asked surprisingly.

"Well, I didn't know that then. Peter never told me till John's death. All I know is that he came back to London a few days before he died. First Mac died and then John. I went to both of their funerals. After the murders of his three brothers, Peter was convinced that he is next and that is exactly what happened."

"Were the deaths of Rob, John and Mac investigated?" Wilfred asked.

"Well, the police are still investigating. But nothing came out yet" said Mr Cunningham.

"Why do you think all of the brothers were murdered? And who can do that? Because you said earlier that you know who killed your friend" Wilfred said.

"At first I didn't know who killed his others brothers but after Pete's death I think I know that this is the work of s single person. But I don't know why they were murdered. The history of the Wood's family can't end like this" said Mr Cunningham.

"Why do you think that one person murdered all of the four brothers?" Wilfred asked?

"Because all of their murder were similar in nature. I think one person did all of this. You have to catch him. I beg of you Mr Dankworth. You are the only person who can solve this mystery" Mr Cunningham said in a pleading voice.

"Did they have any enemies?" Wilfred asked.

"As far as I know there isn't any" Mr Cunningham said.

"Alright now tell me who is the murderer. And you also told me you will say something which will seem a bit unreal. Tell me all of it" Wilfred said.

David Cunningham explained everything thoroughly to Wilfred.

"Is that even possible Mr Cunningham? You are saying that John Woods came out of the grave and murdered rest of his brothers? How in the world this is possible? You said went to his funeral" I said.

"I am saying what I know Mr Bennett. I didn't see John after his death but Pete and his servant Luke did. You can talk to Luke. And yes I went to John's funeral. But one thing all I, Pete and Luke missed out. We couldn't see John's body. We received the news so late and by the time we reached, he was already inside a casket. Detective Wright pointed that out. According to him, that was not John's dead body. He faked his death so that he can kill rest of his brothers. That was someone else's body we buried that day. May be he is right. Because indeed we didn't see John's body. I don't believe in ghosts Mr Dankworth. So from the get going I kept on telling that it is John and he is not dead" Mr Cunningham said.

"Well Mr Cunningham, in that case Police will catch him. They are better than me in this matter" Wilfred said.

"I can understand that Mr Dankworth. But I want to know why he killed rest of his brothers" Mr Cunningham said.

"Alright Mr Cunningham, I am taking this case. I will find out the reason behind these murders" Wilfred said.

The Woods's Castle

I was looking at Wilfred. He seemed a little distracted. David Cunningham left a few minutes ago.

"What is bothering you?" I asked.

"There is a slight possibility but this can't be revenge. Because Brandon Woods kicked out his son out the house. Not his brothers. So if he had to take revenge on anyone it would have been his father. Not his brothers. But his father died right after he left. But he came back to London before he faked his death. So there is a possibility that he already knew about his father's demise. That is why I can't put it as a revenge. There is something else. Something so important that they lost their lives over it" Wilfred said.

"What?" I asked.

"May be they knew something. Something John Woods needed to know. His brothers didn't tell him. So in anguish he killed them all" Wilfred said.

"But tell me one thing, Wilfred. In case it is not the same person, then how will you find who killed Rob Woods? Because he was murdered in Australia" I asked.

"It is the work of one man, Richard. He found them out and then murdered them one by one. We have to go to London. If you want to solve a mystery Richard, start from the root. And in this case the root is Woods's family. We have to start from the royal house. Let me contact Raymond. He is already on the case. So he will know more details than anyone. Let me send a telegram to him" Wilfred said.

"So speak of the devil and the devil arrives?" Raymond asked.

We were sitting at Raymond's apartment. It took three hours to come to London from Wiveliscombe.

"Did someone make contact with you Wilfred? Because I don't think you came all the way to London just by reading the newspaper. So who contacted you?" Raymond asked.

"Have I ever told you that Lestrade never made fun of Sherlock Holmes because he was not that good enough?" Wilfred said laughed out loud.

"Again Wilfred? I told you a million times that do not call me Lestrade. I am better than him" Raymond said in anguish.

"Alright. Then you tell me who came to my house. It was your advice" Wilfred said.

Raymond laughed and said-

"Alright fellows. Enlighten me."

Wilfred described everything to Raymond. Raymond said—

"We spoke to David Cunningham. He told you exactly what he told me. In fact he also lodged a complaint against an officer who was in charge of this case before me. That officer wasn't taking this case seriously. So he was replaced by me. Anyway, how will you start?" Raymond asked.

"We have to go to the Woods's house. I believe everything is there. All we have to do is to find it" Wilfred said.

"Alright. Let's go then" Raymond said.

It was already late in the night. So we decided to go there next morning.

Peter Woods's house wasn't far from Raymond's apartment. It took twenty minutes by car. Well to be honest it wasn't a house exactly. It was like a fortress. The entire area is gigantic. I have never seen any house like this in my entire life. I was mesmerized just by the beauty of the house. The house is a little away from the city area. Perhaps to avoid any chaos which I thought was a brilliant idea. The entire area is surrounded by a ten feet wall. Two police constables were standing at the front gate. They opened the gate as soon as they saw Raymond.

"Goodness gracious me" Wilfred said.

"Yes Wilfred. I said the same words when I came here for the first time" Raymond said with a little smile on his face.

The two sides of the house were covered with trees and beautiful flowers which were looking brighter in the morning sunlight. We stood there for a few minutes just to enjoy the environment and to consume the fresh air of nature. Then we went inside the house.

"Alright Raymond enough to consume the beauty. Let's get to work. You check the ground floor. I and Richard are checking the first. Don't overlook anything" Wilfred said.

We climbed up the stairs. The first floor consisted of four rooms. Each of the rooms had a nameplate at the main door which is rather unusual. Because you don't get to see this very often. Two of the rooms were bedrooms of Peter Woods's and John Woods's. The third one was Peter Woods's study room and the fourth one was the guest room. First we checked Peter Woods's bedroom. His room was perfectly neat and clean.

"What exactly are you looking for here?" I asked.

"Motive. Nobody would kill all of the brothers without any reason. Like I said Richard, that person was looking for something" Wilfred said.

We searched the entire bedroom but we found nothing. So we went to check Peter Woods's study room. The study room was full of books. Different types of books. Wilfred was standing in front of a book shelf. Then he turned his face towards me asked—

"Can you tell me anything unusual looking at these bookshelves?"

"What unusual?" I asked.

"Take a look at yourself" Wilfred said.

So I carefully looked at all of the book slaves but I didn't find anything unusual in particular. So I said—

"No mate. I didn't find anything unusual."

"Ahh Richard. You really disappointed me. You were a soldier, though a long time ago. But still a little bit of your observation power is still left I guess" Wilfred said in a mockery voice as usual.

I got a little angry. I said—

"Why don't you tell me yourself? Because you have clearly seen that I spent at least ten minutes in searching for these book selves while you were enjoying my helplessness sitting on the couch. Come on mate. Please focus on the work."

"Why are you getting angry? I was having a bit of fun" Wilfred laughed and said.

"Making fun of my army life? How many times have I told you that I do not make fun of my past? I served my country with dignity Wilfred and you know that. So I expect an apology" I said in anguish.

"Alright mate. I am sorry. Anyway, what I was trying to tell you is that this room was searched before by someone" Wilfred said.

"What? How can you say that?" I was taken by surprise. Because the entire room was perfectly neat and clean.

"It has been four days since the death of Peter Woods. He was the only person living in this entire house though he has a servant. But he used to go at night. See the date of the table calendar. The date hadn't been changed for the last four days. Now look at the books, the table and the chair. For the last four days nobody lived in this house right? So how on earth is it possible that when nobody lives in the house, the rooms are so neat and clean? It should be full of dirt. Isn't that right mate?" Wilfred asked.

"My God. So the murderer came here and searched the entire house?" I asked.

"Yes my dear Watson. Because I saw footprints on the stairs. I don't know whether you have noticed it or not, all the stairs were covered in dirt. Though the footprints were not clearly visible, but I saw them anyway. And not only that. There is one more thing" Wilfred said.

"What?" I asked.

"The reason why I asked you to look at the books. You did look at them but not properly. Now let me explain. If you see carefully you will find out that all the books are kept in a particular order. Each book self contains same type of books. Look at this one" Wilfred pointed towards a book self.

"This self contains only books about politics and nothing else. The next one contains books about history. Now take a closer look at this self' Wilfred pointed out towards that book self where all of the history books are kept.

"If you look carefully you will find out that among all the history books, one book is about biology. Now it shouldn't be here. It should be on the next book self with all of the other biology books. Now if you take a look at that bookshelf where all the biology books are kept, you will find one history book there. Does that seem normal to you?" Wilfred asked.

"Certainly not" I said.

"Right. This means the murderer searched all the books but in hurry he misplaced them. Forgot to keep them in the right order in right place" Wilfred said.

"Goodness gracious me. But how did he get in? Because the front gate is guarded by the police and the wall is ten feet tall. I am not saying it is impossible to beat the height but he really has to be fit enough to climb this height and then get on the other side" I said.

"I don't think it is impossible for someone to climb a ten feet tall wall who can go to Australia and murder one brother and then come back and murder the rest of the other brothers. Nothing is impossible to them Richard" Wilfred said.

"Alright. Let's search the room" I said.

We searched Peter Woods's study room thoroughly. I was searching all the wardrobes and Wilfred was searching all the books and some other papers.

"My God. Richard look" Wilfred said.

"What?" I almost ran to Wilfred.

He handed me a diary. Something was written there which I didn't understand at all.

"Liam gin mersoset. Lim rried gaian. Ehṛ amne si ifernej. Lwe aveh ughdater. Lyou atsy afes etep."

"What is the meaning of this?" I asked.

There was a slight stroke of smile on Wilfred's face.

"Why are you smiling? My God, have you already found out the meaning?" I asked.

"Yes my dear Watson. Although it doesn't follow a particular pattern but wasn't hard enough. Anyway, let's go to John's room. I got what I needed" Wilfred said.

We went to John Woods's room. And as soon as we entered in his room, Wilfred went towards a photo which was hanging by the wall and stood in front of it with a strange expression.

"It is John Woods's photo isn't it?" Wilfred asked.

"Well it has to be. Because it was his bedroom. But why?" I asked.

"He looks familiar to me" Wilfred said.

"What? Familiar? But how is it possible? Have you ever seen him before?" I asked.

"Of course not. But I don't know why his face" Wilfred didn't end his words. He certainly stopped and then closed both of his eyes.

I wanted to ask him what happened but I didn't. Because I know that these are the moments when he prefers to be left alone and not to be disturbed. So I kept quiet. A few minutes later he opened his eyes and they were brighter than ever. That means he found light in the darkness.

"What is it?" I asked.

"My God Richard. I will explain everything to you. But not now. Let's go" Wilfred said and went out of the room.

"Let's go? Won't you search the room?" I asked.

"That's not needed anymore" Wilfred said.

We both came down to the ground floor. Raymond was standing with a disappointing face. He looked at Wilfred and said—

"I got nothing mate. Have you?"

"Yes I have" Wilfred said and showed that scribble words to Raymond.

"What in the earth is this? It looks like some kind of coded words" Raymond said.

"Well done Lestrade" Wilfred laughed and said.

"Again Wilfred? I told you don't call me Lestrade. I am way better than him. Anyway, did you understand it?" Raymond asked.

"Yes I did. I will explain. But not now. Listen Raymond. I and Richard will go back to Wiveliscombe. Our work is done here. I got what I needed. Now listen to me very carefully. If my doubt is correct, then we don't have much time. Someone's life is in danger" Wilfred said.

"Who's" both I and Raymond asked.

"I told you but not now. Anyway, I will sent you a telegram Raymond. You know what to do after that right?" Wilfred asked.

"Absolutely Poirot" Raymond said.

"For the love of God please don't call me Hercule Poirot. I am nothing in front of that man. Anyway let's go" Wilfred said.

We came out of the house and went through the garden towards the main road. We were about to get on Raymond's car, Certainly Wilfred stopped. He was watching towards an old woman who was also watching Wilfred with a strange look. There were questions in her eyes.

"You go on Raymond. We will find a taxi. Wait for my telegram" Wilfred said and went towards the woman.

Raymond left with his constables.

"Good morning" Wilfred said.

"A very good morning Mr Dankworth" that old lady said.

"Ah. You know me" Wilfred was surprised.

"The entire country know you my son. Especially after you solved the case of Harold Carter and Julia Wilson.

By any chance are you investigating Peter Woods's murder?" that old lady asked.

"Yes madam" Wilfred said.

"Have you ever caught any ghost before Mr Dankworth?" that old lady asked.

"Ghost?" We both asked surprisingly.

"Yes. Because I know who killed Peter Woods" said the old lady.

I and Wilfred both looked at each other.

"Who?" Wilfred asked.

"John Woods" that old lady said.

"What? Are you making fun with us? John Woods died a year ago and Peter Woods himself buried him" I said.

"Yes I know. But he came back from the grave. I saw him in this house a few days ago. He was coming out of the house. I saw his face" that old lay said.

Wilfred looked at her for a while and asked—

"You saw John Woods coming out of the house. Alright. So according to you John Woods's ghost killed Peter Woods?" Wilfred asked.

"Yes. And not only him. His ghost killed rest of his three brothers" that old lady said.

"Don't listen to him. She is mocking with us" I said.

"Just a minute Richard. Are you the only one who saw John Woods or someone else did?" Wilfred asked.

"A few did. Including Peter Woods's servant" that old lady said.

"A servant? We didn't hear about him. I thought he didn't have any servant" Wilfred said.

"What are you doing Wilfred? Mr Cunningham told us about Luke" I whispered into Wilfred's ears.

"Relax Richard. I know what I am doing. Anyway do you know where he lives?" Wilfred asked.

"He lives nearby. Five minutes' walk from here" said that old lady.

"Alright. Can you show us the house?" Wilfred asked.

"Of course I can. Follow me" that old lady said and started walking opposite of the house. We started following her.

After few minutes of walking she pointed towards a house and said—

"Luke lives here. Ask him. He will tell you everything".

"Thank you very much for your help. Have a good day" Wilfred said and went towards the house.

We knocked on the door. A young man opened the door asked—

"May I help you gentlemen?"

"Are you Luke?" Wilfred asked.

"Yes Sir. And you are?" he asked.

"We are investigating Peter Woods's murder. Can we come inside? We have a lot to discuss" Wilfred said.

Luke waited for a few seconds and then said—

"Are any of you Mr Wilfred Dankworth?"

"I am Luke" Wilfred said.

"So Mr Cunningham contacted you. My master told him to do that. Please come inside and take a seat" Luke said.

We came inside sat on a couch. Luke was absolutely devastated just like Mr Cunningham.

"Luke, according to few people Peter Woods was murdered by his Brother John Woods's ghost. Some of them said Peter Woods himself saw his brother's ghost. Is it true?"

"Yes Sir. He was murdered by John Woods but not by his ghost. He didn't die. He faked his death" Luke said.

"We already know that Luke. I was just checking what you believe" Wilfred said.

"At first I didn't believe him. But once both of us were waiting at the garden in the middle of the night. And both of us saw John Woods. And after that a couple of time I saw him going into his house at midnight" Luke said.

"Did you see his face?" Wilfred asked.

"Yes Sir I did. He always carry a torch with him. I saw his face because of that torch" Luke said.

"Can you tell me why he was hunting all of the remaining brothers?" Wilfred asked.

"I don't know that Sir" Luke said.

"Thank you for your help Luke. And by the way, if you remember anything please contact Raymond Right. He is the officer in charge of this case. Have a good day" Wilfred said and we came out to the main road.

"What the hell is going on? If you are not believing in funny ghost stories then why did you interrogate that old lady?" I asked.

"Anything is possible my dear Watson. According to all of us that is John Woods in flesh. But may be one chance in a million that can be John Woods's ghost" Wilfred said.

"Really Wilfred? So now you are going to catch a ghost? Are you serious?" I asked.

"Let's go home first. Then I will explain everything to you including how we will catch the ghost. Alright?" Wilfred said

We were about to catch a taxi but all of a sudden Wilfred pulled my coat. I was taken by surprise.

"What are you doing?" I said and turned towards Wilfred. He was looking on the other side of the road with a frown.

"What is it?" I asked.

"I will tell you later. Alright, listen Richard. I have to stay in London for a reason. You go back to Wiveliscombe and come back to London tomorrow. And don't forget to bring our guns" Wilfred said.

"Guns? You are going to catch him tomorrow? What were you looking at? I asked."

"Have I ever told you Richard you ask lot of questions at a wrong time? Just go back and come tomorrow with our guns" Wilfred said

I know he wanted me to go but I was still standing and looking at him with a lot of questions on my face. I knew he wanted to be alone right now but this time I resisted.

He looked at me and almost screamed—

"What mate?"

I was still looking at his face and he finally realised that he has to tell me something to get rid of me for now.

"Yes I saw something. Something I didn't expect. That's exactly what I was looking at on the other side of the road. But I am not sure whether I am right or not. That's why I can't tell you anything because I have not deducted it yet. It is still in assumption phase. To find out whether I am right or wrong I have to stay here. Seriously Richard you are intolerable. Now please go" Wilfred said.

I threw a smile at him and left with a heart of a lion. Because first time I was able to snatch some information out of him way before he wanted to tell me. I took a taxi and went towards the rail station.

The Unwanted Guest

I reached Wiveliscombe seven in the evening. As I was entering my home, Willie saw me by his window and came running in towards me. That was a bit unexpected.

"Mr Bennett, Mr Bennett" Willie was breathing heavily.

"What happened Willie? You are looking a little worried. Did Evelyn ignored you today?" I asked jokingly.

Willie's face turned red. He looked at me and said—

"Everything is not a joke Mr Bennett. Anyway, if you are not interested then I am leaving" Willie said and were about to leave.

I grabbed his hand said—

"I was joking mate. Why are you getting angry? Let's come inside, take a seat, catch your breath, drink coffee and then tell me what happened. Alright?"

"Of course I will drink coffee seating at your couch Mr Bennett. But this important. Did any one of you came back to Wiveliscombe last night?" Willie asked.

"No. Wilfred is still at London and I came back for some work and will go back to London tomorrow morning. But why are you asking this?"

"I slept late last night. I guess it was around half past one in the night. I was reading a book. I saw someone in Mr Dankworth's kitchen. Someone was standing by the window. You know I have a clear view to Mr Dankworth's kitchen through my bedroom's window. At first I thought it was him. But then I thought it can't be him because he was not as tall as Mr Dankworth. Then I thought I saw it all wrong. So I looked closely but by the time he moved out from there. Approximately twenty minutes later I saw that man again walking out of Mr Dansworth's house. I think someone broke into house Sir while both of you were gone. You should check Mr Bennett" Willie said.

I ran to Wilfred's house and enter from the back door. Because I didn't have the key of his front door. I rushed to his drawing room. Willie was right. Indeed somebody broke into his house. His drawing room was all over the place. And worst of them all, he broke Wilfred's guitar into pieces. I kept everything as it was before. I was a little worried that he might have taken Wilfred's gun. But he didn't. That seemed a little strange to me. Because that man didn't search his bedroom and the gun was there. Anyway I took it and came out of the house.

Willie was still standing outside.

"What happened?" he asked.

"You were right Willie. Somebody broke into his house" I said.

"Did anything got stolen?" he asked.

"I don't think so. But he broke Wilfred's guitar. That will make him mad. Anyway you go back to your home. I will spend the night in Wilfred's house" I said.

The night was eventless as I expected. I drank a lot of coffee to keep myself up throughout the night. In every twenty minutes I roamed his house to check everything is alright.

The next morning I went to London and told Wilfred everything. He was staying at Raymond's house. I gave him the bad news. He jumped out of the bed and the first thing he said—

"Bloody haggard. I am going to kill him."

Raymond was amused by this. He began to laugh. That made Wilfred angrier.

"Why are you laughing?" he asked.

"It is just a guitar mate. There is a lot of guitar shops in London. Buy one from there" Raymond said.

"That guitar was special Raymond. You won't understand" Wilfred said in a rather sadly voice.

"But one thing I didn't understand Wilfred. He searched your drawing room but didn't search your Bedroom. I thought he stole your gun. But the bedroom was intact. I can't figure out why" I said.

"He didn't have the time to search my bedroom. When he was standing at my kitchen, my drawing room was searched by then, for some reason he went to the kitchen. Willie saw him then. But he also saw Willie and got scared of getting caught. He thought Willie will come over and check. That's why he waited twenty minutes for Willie to move out. And when he found out everything was calm. He came out of my house and that's when Willie saw him" Wilfred said.

"But in that twenty minutes he could have searched your bedroom. He had that time" I said.

"Of course he had but he couldn't. Because Willie will come over to check. Now, to search the room he needed to turn on the torch and Willie could have spotted that. That's why he didn't take any risk" Wilfred said.

"But what was he looking for at your house? And who can be that guy" Raymond asked.

"Will find out soon enough mate. Just wait for tonight" Wilfred said.

"Tonight? What is going to happen tonight?" I asked.

"Well I didn't tell you to bring the gun for nothing I guess. Something will go down tonight. And we will be at the middle of it" Wilfred said.

"But how will you catch them" Raymond asked.

"I will lure them in. Look Raymond John Woods is looking for something very much valuable and important to him. He won't let this opportunity go away" Wilfred said.

"But if he realises that it is a trap, then what?" I asked.

"I will try so that he doesn't doubt on my plan that it is a trap. Let's hope he doesn't realise that it is a trap" Wilfred said.

"But where are you intending to catch him?" Raymond asked.

"In Woods's house. If somehow I can let him know that what he is looking for is right there, he will take bate. And that's when we catch them" Wilfred said.

"In that case I have to remove the guards form the gate" Raymond said.

"That will look suspicious Raymond. The landlord just got killed and five days after the killing you take away the guards without solving the case? No Raymond. John Woods is too clever to fell for that. Don't remove them. Instead of standing there the whole night tell them roam around the property from outside in every fifteen minutes. That's the only option we have. You remove the guards the completely, he won't come" Wilfred said.

"So be it. I am going to the station to arrange everything. Do you need extra backup?" Raymond asked.

"I don't think so. We will five including those two guards. I think five people are enough to take one down" Wilfred said.

"Alright, see you later" Raymond went to the station.

"But where we will be waiting?" I asked.

"On the footpath" Wilfred said.

"What? On the footpath? Middle of the night? Are you out of your mind? If he spots us, he will never come. And what about the other people? If they see Wilfred Dankworth, the famous detective, Richard Bennett, the retired army officer and Raymond Wright, the Chief Detective Officer of Scotland Yard are waiting on the footpath in the middle of the night, they will doubt for sure." I said.

"They will doubt only if they recognise us" Wilfred said with a little smile on his face.

"Recognise us means?" I asked.

"We will be wearing makeup my friend. We will dress like a bagger. It will be impossible for anyone to recognise us. In case you haven't noticed, when we came out of the royal house, there was a bagger seating on the footpath. May be a five minutes distance from the house. We will be seating right there waiting for John Woods" Wilfred said.

"But you didn't bring your makeup kit" I said.

"I am going out to buy them. You stay here. I will be back in half an hour" Wilfred said and left.

I could feel excitement in my entire body. I know how dramatic this waiting game can be. Because we did the same thing to catch Harold Carter and Julia Wilson's killer. I took the gun in my hand checked it thoroughly.

"One target, one shot" I murmured.

It was ten past eleven on the night. Wilfred explained everything to Raymond and me. Specially what to do and what not to do. We left the house fifteen minutes before midnight. Half of the city went to sleep. The other half was preparing to go to sleep. Most of the houses went dark. Only the street lights were on. As night fall, the number of people on the road slowly decreased. When we came out we hardly saw anyone walking. It was pretty easy for us. We got off the car ten minutes before the Woods's house and walked the rest of the road. We tried to avoid the street lights and walked through the dark as much as possible. Soon we reached our destination. Wilfred and Raymond inspected the environment first and then we sat under a tree facing the Woods's house. Nothing happened in the first one hour. I was getting restless as usual. But then suddenly Wilfred whispered—

"Fellows. Look straight. Right corner of the road. Do you see anything?" He asked.

We were sitting in the dark for more than an hour. So our eyes were adjusted with the darkness. Though we couldn't see clearly but definitely understood that two people were standing behind a tree. That side was the dark side of the road just like ours.

"Two people? You said this was work of one person" I said.

"I will explain everything Richard. Just focus on the task now" Wilfred said.

The guards were still standing at the gates. Now they moved out of there left the gate unlocked. And as soon as they moved out, the two people enter the garden cautiously. We gave them a three minutes head start and then we moved in. we stood at the gate of the garden for a few minutes. They were still trying to open the main gate of the house. Finally they opened the gate and moved inside. We followed them from a distance. Both of them first searched the ground floor. That was Brandon Woods and his wife Helen Woods's bedroom. They searched there a good ten minutes. We were watching all of these from the outside of the house. Ten minutes later they came out and went upstairs and we followed them there. They both entered Peter Woods's drawing room and started searching the entire room.

Wilfred waited for few minutes and then we all moved in together with gun in our hands—

"You move a muscle and I will shoot you. Stay exactly where you are" Wilfred said.

Both of the criminal froze.

"Turn on the light Richard" Wilfred said.

I turned on all the lights of room.

"Now slowly turned around both of you" Wilfred said.

They both turned around but we couldn't see their faces.

"Do you recognise them Richard and Raymond?" Wilfred asked.

"No. Who are they?" I asked.

"Well he is the one who claimed to be the best friend of late Peter Woods. David Cunningham" Wilfred said.

"Goodness gracious me. Mr Cunningham?" I was shocked.

"And the other one is none other than the old lady from the morning who convinced us that it was John Woods's ghost who killed Peter Woods" Wilfred said.

"So these two killed Peter Woods" Raymond asked.

"No Raymond they didn't kill anybody. They are not capable enough of doing that. They came here for something else. I will explain, but first take them to custody" Wilfred said.

The two guards came and took them away.

"It pretty late. Let's go home. Get some sleep and then I will tell you everything" Wilfred said.

It was seven on the clock in the evening. Wilfred was lying on his couch. I was reading a book about music but my mind was consumed by John Woods's ghost, everything happened last night those code words. Finally I broke the silence—

"Will you kindly tell me what exactly happened last night? How in the world David Cunningham and that old lady have to do with Peter Woods's murder. He was the one who bought the case to us. Then what was he doing in the Royal house with that old lady in the middle of the night? I deserve to know mate. You told everything to Raymond. Then why keep me in the darkness?" I asked.

"I didn't tell Raymond everything Richard. I am still solving the puzzle. Unless I connect everything in a straight line, it is not going to be easy for me to say anything. Now how they are connected to this entire case? Well, that's a mystery even I am having difficulty to solve. I guess I have to dig a little deep to get to the bottom of this" Wilfred said.

"Alright. But at least you can tell me the meaning of that code word you found at Woods's house" I said.

"Of course mate. Why not? Take a look" Wilfred said and handed me that piece of paper.

Then he said—

"I told you earlier that it doesn't follow any particular pattern but it was easy to break. Read those words again."

"Liam gin mersoset. Lim rried gaian. Ehr amne si ifernej. Lwe aveh ughdater. Lyou atsy afes etep" I read them loudly.

"Now do as I tell you. Let's take the first line. 'Liam gin mersoset.' Now you know that it doesn't mean anything. Now Liam is a name but in this case it is not. Remove the letter 'L'. So the remaining word is 'iam' which is 'I am'. Do you get it?" Wilfred asked.

"My God. And the rest?" I asked.

"'gin mersoset' is remove 'g' and you get 'in'. 'mersoset' is nothing but 'Somerset'. The alphabets were mixed with each other. So the entire line becomes 'I am in Somerset'." Wilfred said.

"Goodness gracious me Wilfred. You are a genius" I said.

"So the meaning of the entire piece is—

'Liam gin mersoset. Lim rried gaian. Ehr amne si ifernej. Lwe aveh ughdater. Lyou atsy afes etep'

'I am in Somerset. I married again. Her name is Jenifer. We have a daughter. You stay safe Pete.'

'Lim rried' is 'I married'. Again remove the 'L' add 'm' with the next word. If you keep on going like this, you will understand the entire meaning" Wilfred said.

"So this letter was written by their father, Mr Brandon Woods?" I asked.

"Yes. Most probably after leaving his house" Wilfred said.

"He came here in Somerset. And he married again and they had a daughter. How old will she be now? If she is still alive" I asked.

"This letter was written a long time ago. Perhaps she will be in between twenty five and thirty and she is alive for sure" Wilfred said.

"So her life is in danger? You were talking about her earlier weren't you?" I asked.

"Yes Richard. And most probably she is in Somerset. We have to find her before John Woods does" Wilfred said.

"But why will John Woods try to kill her?" I asked.

"As far as I have understood by connecting all of these incidents, John Woods is looking for something. Something very much important to him. And he wants to relish that alone. He doesn't want to share that with anyone else. I believe that thing which he wants so badly belongs to his father. That's why he killed his three brothers and now if he knows about the girl child, he will kill her too. Because she is the only one remaining who can claim what John Woods wants. This is the only explanation I have right now" Wilfred said.

I took a deep breath and said—

"It is enough. This is exactly what is happening. But how will you find her?"

"Well, I think I have a clue but it is just my imagination. I can't prove it now, I need some time. If my doubt is true. I will find her easily. Anyway, let me play some music" Wilfred said and started playing his bluesy music as usual.

I was about to leave but Wilfred stopped me in the half way—

"I am going back to London. But you stay here. That girl is here Richard. I don't know how you will recognise her but at least try. I will come back within two days."

The Last Descendant

These two days were eventless. I tried to find Brandon Woods's daughter. But it was an impossible task for me. Because I don't have Wilfred's detection power. I woke up a little early next morning and was pretty much surprised to see Willie talking to Wilfred. Once Willie left I went outside.

"It is very strange to see that Willie was talking to you" I said.

"Yes it is. But if we are living in the same place we better get to know each other. Anyway, come to my home. We have a lot to discuss" Wilfred said went towards his house.

I went inside. Freshen up and went to Wilfred's house.

"Yes Wilfred?" I asked.

"I found that girl" Wilfred said.

"What? When?" I asked. It was a bolt from the blue.

"Last night. I came back to Wiveliscombe around eleven in the night, I waited for you to sleep and then did some investigation on my own" Wilfred said.

"Without even telling me? I could have gone with you" I said.

"Yes you could have but you were tired. Remember? So I didn't want to bother you. Anyway, listen. I just sent a telegram to Raymond. He is coming as early as possible. Take a good nap this afternoon. Because we have to stay awake tonight" Wilfred said.

"For what?" I asked.

"To catch John Woods's ghost" Wilfred said.

"Again? Ghost? That thing doesn't exist, Wilfred. It is John Woods. He didn't die. There is no ghost in this. And now he is taking revenge on his brothers. But how will you catch him?" I asked.

"He will come. He has to" Wilfred said.

"Alright. Who is the girl?" I asked.

"Tonight. Not now" Wilfred said.

I spent the rest of the day lying on Wilfred's couch. As night was approaching, I was getting restless. Because I had no idea what was about to happen. Around eight o'clock in the evening Raymond came with four constables.

"They are waiting exactly where you told them to wait" Raymond said.

"And the others?" Wilfred asked.

"They are in the car with four more constables" Raymond said.

"Right. Well we have to wait for three more hours. We will leave at eleven o clock" Wilfred said.

Ten past eleven on the clock. I, Wilfred and Raymond came out of our house very quietly and started walking towards the river side.

"At least tell me where we are going" I said.

"You will see soon enough. Just wait for a while" Wilfred said.

Within twenty minutes we reached in front of a house.

"Please tell me what's going on Wilfred" I said.

"Quiet. Not now" Wilfred said.

We didn't have to wait long. It was ten past twelve on the clock. I almost fell asleep but woke up because of Wilfred.

"What is it?" I asked.

Raymond pointed his finger towards the road. My entire body shook as soon as I saw where Raymond was pointing. A man, around six feet tall, wearing a black overcoat, and a black hat was slowly approaching the house.

"Is that?" I asked.

"John Woods. Not the ghost but in the flesh." Wilfred said.

"So what are you waiting for Wilfred? Catch him" I said.

"Not now. Let him get inside the house. We will go after him" Wilfred said.

John Woods waited for a few seconds and then went inside the house. We also waited for a few minutes and then we too entered the house following him. First we reached the drawing room. Although it was dark inside, still we could see John Woods pretty clearly. He took out a knife from his pocket and went towards the bedroom. He slowly opened the door. A girl was sleeping on the bed. She had no idea that a man was standing beside her bed with a knife in his hand. I grabbed Wilfred's hand.

"Do something mate" I whispered into Wilfred's ear.

As John Woods was about to stab the girl, Raymond turned on the lights. He was taken by surprise but soon realised that he fell into a trap. He tried to throw the knife towards Raymond but he couldn't. Before he could have thrown the knife, Wilfred jumped on him and punched him right on his face. He was knocked out. The girl woke up because of this chaos and was absolutely stunned watching all of us inside her bedroom. I couldn't believe my eyes.

The girl was Evelyn. Our Evelyn Foster. Brandon Woods's only daughter.

"What is going on? Mr Dankworth? Mr Bennett? And who is this man?" Evelyn asked.

"I will explain everything Evelyn. Just wait. Get him up Raymond and bring him to the drawing room" Wilfred said.

A Murderer in Flesh Not in Spirit

We all went to the drawing room.

"You look exactly like your father in this makeup. But you forgot one thing. Even without makeup there is a huge similarity between you and your father Mr Roger Woods also known as our good neighbour Mr Willie Brooke" Wilfred said.

I just felt an out of body experience.

"Willie Brooke? Our Willie" I asked.

"Yes my dear Richard. Our Willie. He is the only son of John Woods. Raymond kindly pulled out his false beard and his moustache" Wilfred said.

Raymond pulled out his makeup and I closed my eyes in sadness and disappointment. I couldn't believe my eyes. This is the man with whom I spent almost every morning in my garden talking with each other. And now he is a cold blooded murderer?

We all gathered in Evelyn's drawing room. We mean I, Wilfred, Raymond, Evelyn and Willie with three constables. Wilfred was waiting.

"Are you waiting for someone?" I asked.

"Yes David Cunningham and that old lady. They need to be here. Because there is a lot to talk about" Wilfred said.

David Cunningham and that old lady arrived ten minutes later and then Wilfred started to unfold the mystery—

"To understand whatever has happened, we have to go way back in history. This started a long time ago inside the Woods's family. The Woods family was one of the oldest royal families in England. The head of the family was Late Brandon Woods and her wife Helen Woods. They had four sons. Rob Woods, the eldest one, Mac Woods, John Woods and Peter Woods, the youngest one. All the brothers were very much polite except John Woods. He was rough and rude. There was an incident which took place at the anniversary of Brandon and Helen Woods. The entire family was celebrating when John Woods misbehaved with a waitress of the house. As a result he was punished badly by his father and kicked out of the house. He took the punishment very seriously and in angriness he left the house and never came back though his father didn't mean it. His mother couldn't tolerate this incident. So a few days after her son's departure she died. And a few years later their heart broken father left the house but he never told anyone where he had gone.

A few years later Brandon Woods sent a coded letter to his son Peter Woods telling him about his whereabouts. After that all the murder began. Rob Woods died first. He was in Australia at the time of his death. He was living there for his occupational purpose. He was murdered brutally. The Australian police did investigate but couldn't catch the killer. Right after Rob Woods's demise, Mac Woods was murdered in the same fashion. Exactly one year later John Woods was found dead in London. He was murdered just like his elder brother. But for some reason he came back to London. No one knew why. Not even Peter Woods. And then few days ago Peter Woods was brutally murdered at the Regent's park. This man, Mr David Cunningham brought this case to me. He was a friend of Peter Woods. According to him John Woods killed all the other brothers for a purpose. He also believed that it is a work of one man.

So I started my investigation. I went to London. I always believed that if you want to find something, then start from the root. And in this case the root was the Woods's castle. While searching Peter Woods's study room, I came across that coded letter. It said—

'Liam gin mersoset. Lim rried gaian. Ehr amne si ifernej. Lwe aveh ughdater. Lyou atsy afes etep'

And the meaning of this coded letter is—

'I am in Somerset. I married again. Her name is Jenifer. We have a daughter. You stay safe Pete.'

That means after leaving Woods's castle Brandon Woods came to Somerset and married a woman named Jenifer. They had a girl child. Now, I didn't know that girl child is Evelyn until last night. I will explain how. Now, after understanding the meaning of this letter I went to search John Woods's bed room. And as soon as I entered, one particular thing grabbed my attention. It was a photo of John Woods hanging from the wall. He looked familiar to me. It seemed I saw him before or someone looked like him. But right after that I realised why his face looked familiar to me. Let me show you. Please bring the photo Raymond".

Raymond took out the photo of John Woods from the bag. Then Wilfred covered the entire face of John Woods except his eyes and his forehead and then said—

"Now see the similarity yourself."

We were stunned. The eyes and the forehead of Roger Woods look exactly like John Woods.

Wilfred said—

"Right then and there I understood who killed all of the four brothers. And if he is in Somerset Wiveliscombe, then that girl also has to be here."

"But why did he disguise himself?" I asked.

"This is where this two persons come in. After leaving London, John Woods went to Lancashire. He was a son of Royal family. He was privileged and never faced any difficulty in his life. But this time it was a completely different scenario. He came to Lancashire with little bit of money and clothes. As I said he was a privileged child, he didn't know how save money for future. His luxury life continued there till he went bankrupt. He was the son of Brandon Woods.

Everybody recognised him there. So they offered him work to survive. This is when John Woods saw a terrible poverty. He was struggling. This life of his made him a changed man. He finally realised all of his mistakes and his wrong doings. He started going to the church regularly and asked for forgiveness from the Lord. All of his anguish and wish of taking revenge on his father melted in his tears. He finally realised the value of life.

Slowly he came in terms that he is not the part of the royal family anymore and this his home now. So he started to build a new life. He married a woman. Maria Dawson. Later Maria Woods" Wilfred said and turned towards that old lady.

"My God" said Raymond.

Wilfred started again—

"But there was a problem. Maria is not exactly as she looks. She is greedy and had or to be honest still has a habit of stealing things from people's house. That didn't stop even after her marriage. Soon they were blessed by a child. Roger Woods. Roger grew up listening to the stories about the royal family and the past of his father and idealised his father's past as his present. So as he grew up, he turned into rough, reckless and a rude child. John Woods tried to contain him but failed. Because his mother would encourage him to be like this."

Now why did he disguised himself? To stay hidden in the dark. Roger knew about the past of his father. That his father was a very rough and rude person. And he left the house at a very young age in anguish. So he decided to use that as a weapon. Instead of confronting his uncles with his own appearance, he decided to come in the disguise of his father. Because he knew everybody will believe that John Woods is taking revenge because of the past incident. First he killed Rob and Mac. Then I believe he killed his father too. Isn't that right Willie? Oh sorry mate. I should call you Roger. You killed your father didn't you?" Wilfred asked.

Willie couldn't speak a word. His hands were shaking.

"Alright. Let me tell them. Yes Roger. You killed your father. As you were growing up your father told you something very much important and were hidden from most of the people in the royal family. As soon as you heard it you told this to your mother. Both you and your mother forced him to say its whereabouts but I guess he denied. So you and your mother made a plan. A plan with Mr David Cunningham" Wilfred said.

"What?" I almost screamed. There was pin drop silence in the room.

"Yes Richard. Just like Maria Woods, David Cunningham is not exactly what he looks. He always told us that he was the best friend of Peter Woods. But that was not entirely two. He had another friend. John Woods. And they were very much close. So when John left London, David Cunningham was hurt but didn't show this to anyone. Later stages of his life he started his journey to find John and he did find him in

Lancashire But by the time he found John, he was a different man. Roger grew up and already forcing his father about that precious thing. He and his mother told Mr Cunningham about that thing. Perhaps he also asked John Woods to give up the information but just like earlier John Woods denied. So they made a plan of scaring John Woods by killing two of his brothers."

"David Cunningham's duty was to find the whereabouts the brothers and Roger did the rest. First he killed Rob Woods in Australia and then Mac Woods in England. After hearing his brother's death John Woods realised who did the killings and wanted to save his last brother Peter Woods. Because he knew he would die. So he came to London quietly but couldn't escape the eyes of David Cunningham. The news reached Roger and his mother and they followed him to London. But before John Woods even talk to his brother, Roger Woods killed his father in cold blood. And not only that. Somehow he delayed the news of his father's death from reaching Peter Woods. So by the time Peter Woods knew about his brother's death, John Woods were already put inside the casket. Peter Woods, his servant Luke and David Cunningham were present at John Woods's funeral. So they didn't see his body.

After this Roger would dress like his father and started to scare Peter Woods. The motive was to bring him out of the house and snatch the information about that precious thing. The plan worked definitely but not entirely. Peter Woods did come out of his house and met Roger in the Regents Park in the middle of the night. But just like his brother he too declined to give up the information. So Roger killed him and then somehow found out that his grandfather Brandon Woods was married again and he had a daughter. So he and David Cunningham started to search the entire country and finally they found her here. Though none of them were sure that Evelyn is the girl but they had a doubt. I am an old resident Wiveliscombe. I clearly remember when Roger also known as Willie came into my neighbourhood. It was not long ago. Now will you kindly bother to tell us why you killed your father and your uncles?" Wilfred asked.

"No? You won't? Alright mate. Allow me. I did some digging about Woods's' family and I came across a news. Woods's family was one the oldest, most respected and loved family in the entire country. Despite their royal status, they always maintained a very good relation with the people from the very beginning. This generous behaviour won the heart of the king of England at that time. As a result the king of England presented a big amount of his treasure to Brandon Woods's grandfather Tyrion Woods. But Tyrion thought that if this treasure falls into wrong hands that will be catastrophic. So he decided to hide it. Only Brandon Woods, his son, knew about this treasure. And before leaving the house, he told his youngest son about it.

Now this type of news doesn't stay hidden for a long time. I believe during the stories by mistake John

Woods told him or somehow he came across this news and asked his father about this. I believe his father simply denied its existence or simply said I know nothing about this. But this didn't impress Roger Woods. And in anguish he killed his father and three uncles. Isn't that right Mr Woods?" Wilfred asked.

Roger Woods slowly nodded his head.

"Now tell everybody how did you find Evelyn and how did you get to know about her? Come on speak up" Wilfred said those last words loudly.

"Uncle Peter told me that my grandfather was married again and they had a daughter. But he didn't tell me where my grandfather went. But it wasn't hard to speculate where he could have gone. The Woods's castle was built a little outside of the city. That means he was a peaceful man. So wherever he had gone, that place had to be quiet. So I started searching in countryside and about a year ago I saw Evelyn here. Her eyes are exactly like my father's. Right then I realised that she is the daughter of Brandon Woods. I told this to my mother and Mr Cunningham. They were not sure that Evelyn is the girl. So they asked me to shift to Wiveliscombe. But I couldn't kill her. Because I had to know where the treasure was. She was the only one who could have led me to the treasure. So I made friendship with her. And despite the similarity, she never realised that I am her father's grandson" Roger said.

"But you still don't know where the treasure is right?" Wilfred asked.

"Yes" Roger replied.

"Then why did you try to kill Evelyn?" I asked.

"Because I was afraid. Mr Dankworth already started the investigation. I thought his instinct could have led him to me. So I wanted to clear my path" Roger said.

"So you wanted to clear your path. How wonderful. But did you clear your path Roger? I don't think so. Your delinquency just set a new path for you. A path to jail. Take him away Raymond" Wilfred said.

It was early morning. I, Wilfred and Evelyn were standing at Evelyn's garden. She asked—

"Now please tell me how you knew I am Brandon Woods's daughter."

In reply Wilfred handed her a photo.

"How did you get this?" Evelyn asked.

"I am so sorry Evelyn. I broke into your house last night when you weren't home. That's when I found it" Wilfred said.

"But how did you guess that I could be that girl?" she asked.

"In the same way Roger understood. Your eyes. They are just like your father's. I wasn't sure until I saw the photo" Wilfred said.

"Can I see it?" I asked.

"Oh. Absolutely" Evelyn said.

It was a photo of Evelyn standing with Brandon Woods and her mother Jenifer Woods.

"I guess Evelyn is not your real name. Is it?" Wilfred asked.

"No Sir. It is Charlotte. Charlotte Woods" Evelyn said.

"Let's go for a walk. I need some fresh air. Let's go to the river side" Wilfred said.

"Yes, that will be a very good idea" Evelyn also known as Charlotte Woods said.

We came back from London a while ago. Wilfred went to the biggest guitar shop in the city and bought one. We were sitting on his drawing room. He was checking out the guitar thoroughly. Though I was trying to concentrate on a book but I couldn't due to some unanswered questions in my mind. So I finally opened up—

"I know you are little busy but can I ask you something?" I said.

"I am always free for you Hastings. You want to know how I found out that David Cunningham was involved in this and that old lady is Willie or Roger's mother, don't you" Wilfred said.

I couldn't control my laughing. Because this is exactly what I was thinking. I said—

"Yes Wilfred. Now please tell me how."

"Do you remember what I did when we came to the main road after talking to Luke in London?" Wilfred asked.

"Yes. Clearly. You pulled my hand and were looking at the other side of the road very carefully. You even had a frown" I said.

"Exactly. My eyes were stuck on a person. By his walking he seemed very much familiar to me but he looked different. So I told you to go back to Wiveliscombe and I followed that man to his house. There was a nameplate on his front gate and it had a name written there. David Cunningham. I was shocked watching this. The only reason I didn't recognise him because he was under disguise. That was the first time I had a hunch that he might be involved. Now you can argue that because of all these killings he is wearing makeup to keep himself safe. If that was the case, then he should wear it when he came to Wiveliscombe. But he came without makeup. This is why I thought that he might be involved in this. So I played a card.

I told Raymond the entire thing and sent a constable to his house with a letter. It was written that the police have identified why all these killings happened. What John Woods is looking for is somewhere in the Woods's house. The police will start searching the entire house a day after tomorrow. Well I did this by my hunch. Just wanted to how he reacts to it. And it worked. He walked right into the trap. Well, till then I didn't know that old lady is Maria Woods and she is also involved. I only set the trap for David

Cunningham. Once they get caught, Raymond interrogated them. That old lady confessed that she is John Woods's wife Maria Woods but never told that his husband died and the one who is doing all the killings is his son.

Even David Cunningham denied to say anything. That's why I needed to go to Lancashire. Because by then I knew that they are the helping hands of the killer. I had to find the root. I don't know if you still remember or not, when David Cunningham visited out place, he said that he spent quite a few time in Lancashire. Now why somebody would go to Lancashire from London without any reason? That is when it struck my mind that he went to Lancashire in search of John Woods. So how the equation stands? He said that Peter Woods was his best friend and he had good relation with his brothers. Now one thing I didn't realise then is that he never criticised John Woods. All he said that the people and other family members of the Woods's family criticised him. He himself never said a word against John Woods.

Once I realised that, I was sure that he went to Lancashire in search of him. So I went to Lancashire and gathered all this information. There I got to know that John Woods was married and he had a son name Roger Woods. Now if you remember, when I saw John Woods's photo in the Royal house, I said that he looks similar to someone. Someone I know. Right there I realised that a part of his face looks exactly like Willie's. That's when I started doubting. But when I got to know that John Woods had a son, I was absolutely sure that his son is none other than our neighbour Willie.

Now by the coded letter we already knew that Brandon Woods was married again and he had a daughter. So that means that girl has a claim on the same thing for what Willie was killing his uncles including his father. So if Willie is in Wiveliscombe, then that girl has to be in Wiveliscombe. Because Willie is here for quite a long time. So if the girl is not a resident of Wiveliscombe, then why would Willie spend this much time here? Simple equation isn't it? Now the question was who that can be? Well the answer was easy. Evelyn" Wilfred said.

"But how is that easy? Please explain" I said.

"Because Willie has a huge interest on Evelyn" Wilfred said.

"I laughed out loud and said—

"I guess almost every man in Wiveliscombe has interest on Evelyn."

"You are absolutely right Richard. But there is a difference. Take yourself as an example. You have interest on Evelyn right? So just try to remember what kind of activity you do to impress her. You even wrote a romantic poem for her. Now almost every man in Wiveliscombe who has interest on Evelyn, does some kind of activity to impress her. That's quite normal. But have you ever seen Willie to do any activity like this?" Wilfred asked.

My God. He is right. Willie didn't.

"All Willie did is spoke to her once or twice a day. Because Willie understood that Evelyn's eyes were similar to his father's. John Woods had that same similarity so does Willie or Roger Woods. So Willie showed interest on Evelyn to make sure that Evelyn is Brandon Woods's daughter. But once he found out that I am investigating, he got scared. David Cunningham came to my house. He definitely had seen him coming. Well, that was not part of the plan. But because Peter Woods himself said to David Cunningham in front of Luke that if he dies David Cunningham should come to me. And Raymond also said the same thing. So he had no choice but to come to me. Otherwise Luke would have.

This scared Willie. So he was in hurry. Because he knew about my detection and deduction ability. So he played a trick though it didn't work. He broke into my house and destroyed my drawing room and broke my guitar. He had ample time to steal my gun. But that was not the part of the plan. The plan was to distract me. I would care so much about my guitar rather than my gun. So he only broke my guitar. And then once you came back he himself said to this you to keep himself safe. So that we don't doubt on him. But like I said that didn't work. So he got desperate. He decided to kill Evelyn and search the house for the treasure. That's all" Wilfred stopped.

"But how did you get to know about the treasure?" I asked.

"Through the British Government. I help them in their cases. So I asked for a favour. They gave me that information" Wilfred said.

"Goodness me. It didn't look that complicated at the beginning. Any way I am going. I have a story to write. Second adventure of Wilfred Dankworth" I said.

"Have you thought a name yet?" Wilfred asked.

"Yes. The man from the grave" I said.

Wilfred smiled and said—

"That's a good name mate."

About the Author

Satanik Basu

Satanik Basu, a post graduate in Computer Science and Application and a guitarist by profession was born in 1st February 1989 in Kolkata, India. His love for books began when he was 12 years old. Detective, crime and thriller became his favourite genres and still are now. His first ever book was published in the International Kolkata Book fair 2022 under the publication house "The Cafe Table", a Kolkata based publisher. Since then he published two more books from Ukiyoto publishing house. All in thrilller category. He also participated in two creative writing competition where he ranked 50 and 73 in the country.

www.ingramcontent.com/pod-product-compliance
Lightning Source LLC
LaVergne TN
LVHW091612170726
843492LV00007B/2364